A Note to Parents and Caregivers:

Read-it! Readers are for children who are just sarting on the amazing road to reading. These beautiful books supp the acquisition of reading skills and the love of books.

The PURPLE LEVEL presents basic g high frequency words and simple langua.

The RED LEVEL presents fammon words and repeating sentence pat.

The BLUE LEVEL presents new ideg a larger vocabulary and varied sentence structure.

The YELLOW LEVEL presents more challenging ideas, a broad vocabulary, and wide variety in sentence structure.

The GREEN LEVEL presents more complex ideas, an extended vocabulary range, and expanded language structures.

The ORANGE LEVEL presents a wide range of ideas and concepts using challenging vocabulary and complex language structures.

When sharing a book with your child, read in short stretches, pausing often to talk about the pictures. Have your child turn the pages and point to the pictures and familiar words. And be sure to reread favorite stories or parts of stories.

There is no right or wrong way to share books with children. Find time to read with your child, and pass on the legacy of literacy.

Adria F. Klein, Ph.D.
Professor Emeritus
California State University
San Bernardino, California

Editor: Patricia Stockland
Storyboarder: Amy Bailey Muehlenhardt
Page Production: Melissa Kes/JoAnne Nelson/Tracy Davies
Art Director: Keith Griffin
Managing Editor: Catherine Neitge
The illustrations in this book were done in acrylic.

Picture Window Books
5115 Excelsior Boulevard
Suite 232
Minneapolis, MN 55416
877-845-8392
www.picturewindowbooks.com

Printed in the United States of America.

Library of Congress Cataloging-in-Publication Data
Blair, Eric.
The Legend of Daniel Boone / by Eric Blair ; illustrated by Micah Chambers-Goldberg.
p. cm. — (Read-it! readers: tall tales)
Summary: Relates episodes from the life of Daniel Boone, a talented hunter and woodsman
who helped explore the American West.
ISBN 1-4048-0974-0 (hardcover)
1. Boone, Daniel, 1734-1820—Juvenile literature. 2. Pioneers—Kentucky—Biography—
Juvenile literature. 3. Frontier and pioneer life—Kentucky—Juvenile literature.
4. Kentucky—Biography—Juvenile literature. [1. Boone, Daniel, 1734-1820. 2. Pioneers.
3. Frontier and pioneer life.] I. Chambers-Goldberg, Micah, ill II. Title. III. Read-it!
readers tall tales.
F454.B66B57 2004
976.9'02'092—dc22
2004018440

The Legend
of Daniel Boone

By Eric Blair

Illustrated by Micah Chambers-Goldberg

Special thanks to our advisers for their expertise:

Adria F. Klein, Ph.D.
Professor Emeritus, California State University
San Bernardino, California

Susan Kesselring, M.A.
Literacy Educator
Rosemount-Apple Valley-Eagan (Minnesota) School District

PICTURE WINDOW BOOKS
Minneapolis, Minnesota

Daniel Boone was born in a log cabin in Pennsylvania.

One day, Daniel threw a diaper pin across the room and hit his bottle. Daniel's parents knew that he would be a great hunter.

To be a good hunter, Daniel needed
many skills.

Skillful Indians near the Boone farm taught young Daniel to move silently through the forest.

Daniel learned to track and trap wild animals. He also learned to fish.

Daniel hunted deer, bears, and wild birds for his family to eat.

Daniel hunted with knives
and tomahawks.

He could throw them farther than other men could see.

As Daniel grew, his adventures grew.
Once, he wrestled with a
huge grizzly bear
for three days.

On the third day, the bear gave up
and went back to its cave.

Daniel's older brother thought the young hunter needed more than knives and tomahawks.

So, he made Daniel a long rifle.
Daniel named the gun Tick Licker.

With his new rifle, Daniel could shoot a tick off a deer without even ruffling the animal's fur.

From 300 steps away, Daniel could
shoot an acorn out of a tree.

Later, Daniel decided to move
to the West.

There were no easy roads to get there. So, Daniel followed the path of the Indians and buffalo.

Daniel wanted other people to move west.

So, he got fifteen men with axes.
Together, they cleared the trail for
more settlers.

Soon, pioneers were headed west on Daniel Boone's Wilderness Road.

The road wasn't always safe from animals and thieves. Sometimes, Daniel would hide in the trees to protect the pioneers.

He would shoot at bears and bandits
to scare them away.

One day, Daniel saw two blue eyes in the forest. He'd never seen an animal with blue eyes.

The eyes belonged to a girl named
Rebecca. She loved the wild as much
as Daniel did.

Daniel and Rebecca decided
to get married.

BOONE

They built a log cabin in the West
and lived happily ever after.

More *Read-it!* Readers

Bright pictures and fun stories help you practice your reading skills. Look for more books at your level.

TALL TALES

Annie Oakley, Sharp Shooter by Eric Blair

John Henry by Christianne C. Jones

Johnny Appleseed by Eric Blair

The Legend of Daniel Boone by Eric Blair

Paul Bunyan by Eric Blair

Pecos Bill by Eric Blair

Looking for a specific title or level? A complete list of *Read-it!* Readers is available on our Web site:
www.picturewindowbooks.com

4:31